DESI

IRMA VLADI

DESI

Fairy tale

IRMA VLADI. DESI

A beautifully illustrated fairy tale for children 6-10 years old. A heartwarming story about friendship, love, and faithfulness. The main characters are a boy and a girl who live in a small town and are good friends from early childhood. Suddenly, their peaceful life turns into tribulation, and going through challenges, children learn how to make the right choice and protect their friendship and love.

PRINTED IN THE UNIDED STATES OF AMERICA

First Edition

Library of Congress Cataloging-in-Publication Data
LCCN 2020909099

ISBN: 978-1-7348742-0-4

This story happens once upon a time in a land where the fields are golden, the woods are green, and the rivers are blue. In this wonderful land, the sun shines during the day, and at night, the moon and stars pour down silver light.

Amongst the meadows, there is a tiny town. Little Town is its name. People who live there use their talents to help each other. Carpenters build beautiful homes, bakers make tasty bread, and shoemakers sew comfortable shoes. Life in Little Town is pleasant because everyone is joyful. Travelers enjoy visiting this place, as they always find hospitable inhabitants, good food, and cozy rooms available for guests.

The most popular place in Little Town is Central Square, a small square with a fountain surrounded by flowers. Townspeople come here to celebrate holidays, to exchange news on weekends, and occasionally to announce something important.

Nearby, there is a tavern named the Fifth Wheel. Tim, the owner, is a kind person, and his cuisine is the best in town. A pilgrim can always find shelter there.

This is the moment when our story begins...

One rainy and breezy evening, a stranger knocks on the door of the Fifth Wheel. Tim opens the door, and a lady in a long raincoat with a big hood covering her head walks inside.

"May I have a meal and a room for the night?" she asks.

"Dinner is ready, and a nice room with a view of the lake awaits you, Miss," answers Tim.

The lady takes off her coat, and Tim sees how attractive she is. Golden curls surround a thin face, her body has the shape of an ancient statue, and her long fingers end with pretty nails. The dress she wears is made of expensive fabric that only wealthy people have.

"What is your name, Miss?" Tim says to the lady.

"My name is Desi."

"Desi? What a beautiful name!"

"My true name is Desire, but Desi is what I like to be called."

"How long are you planning to stay in our town?"

"I don't know. I have to wait for my escort to join me."

As Desi speaks these words, the storm becomes stronger. The rain turns into a downpour, a flash of lightning illuminates the room, and thunder rattles the windows.

By midnight, everything becomes quiet, the moon and stars come out from behind the clouds, and the sky becomes clear again.

At dawn, the birds sing louder than usual. Sunrise starts a bright new day after the dark and stormy night.

In a small house at the edge of the town live a boy and a girl named Kai and Mia. They live with Mia's grandmother, who is the best grandma in the whole world. The children like to spend time together. People often see them playing or working in the garden in front of the house. Mia and Kai take good care of all the plants. Roses are their favorites. Three big rosebushes with red, white, and yellow flowers bloom from spring till autumn, spreading around a sweet fragrance. At the peak of the season, the children make small bouquets and give them to their neighbors.

This morning, Mia wakes up early. She opens her eyes, looks through the window, and sees an oriole sitting on a lilac branch and singing.

"It is you who is not letting me sleep!" Mia says to the bird. She opens the window, and fresh air with the aroma of the lilac blossoms fills the room. Mia dresses quickly and runs to the garden to check the roses after the storm. She finds them unmarred and freshly covered with raindrops. Mia touches the flowers and breathes in their fragrance. At the same moment, she smells something from the kitchen. Grandma always wakes up before the children and makes breakfast for them. Mia runs back into the house and knocks on Kai's door.

"Get up quickly, you lazybones! Breakfast is waiting!" Mia says to Kai through the door.

Kai opens his eyes and looks at the wall clock. "Oh! It is not even seven! I can sleep for another hour," he murmurs.

"You will Miss all the exciting things!" says Mia laughing.

"OK, I will get up right away then," says Kai.

At this time, in the Fifth Wheel, Tim serves breakfast to the guests.

Desi is still asleep. Her room is dark because the shutters are closed. A ray of sun, coming from a gap between the shutters, crawls across the pillow and touches Desi's face. Immediately, she opens her eyes.

"Oh! The sun is so bright!" Desi says to herself. She closes her eyes for a moment and then opens them again. "I slept so well last night!" she says in a happy voice. She gets out of bed, dresses, and goes downstairs.

"Good morning, Miss! Would you like to have breakfast here or in your room?" Tim asks Desi.

"Good morning! Usually, I don't have breakfast so early," says Desi. "What can I see in your town?"

"The most picturesque spot is Central Square. It is not far from here. But all the shops and restaurants are closed right now. Most of the townspeople are in the Cathedral. Everything will open after the service ends."

"Thank you."

Desi steps outside and follows a narrow street that leads to Central Square. She finds the street beautiful. All the little houses look like artworks; each has a tiny garden full of pretty flowers. Desi comes to the square and finds it empty, with no one around. She takes a seat on the bench near the fountain, closes her eyes, and listens to the sounds of the water.

"Oh! It's so peaceful here," she says.

This morning in Kai and Mia's house, grandma is making pancakes. The children love pancakes. They enjoy them even more with a jam made from wild raspberries. Now, Kai and Mia are sitting at the table and waiting for grandma to finish her cooking. Finally, she takes the last pancake from the pan and brings the whole stack to the table. Kai instantly grabs two for his plate and covers them with jam.

"Look at you, sweet tooth!" exclaims Grandma, "Eat your porridge first!"

"I hate porridge!" grouses Kai.

"Porridge makes you strong!" says Grandma and puts a full bowl in front of him.

"I love porridge!" Mia says. "I would have more if we didn't have pancakes."

"Kids, don't forget to drink your milk!"

They quickly finish the meal, and while Kai washes the dishes, Mia goes outside to feed the birds. Every morning, she sprinkles millet and breadcrumbs on the ground, and many kinds of birds fly to the garden. One bird, a white dove with a black spot on her head, is Mia's favorite.

The girl calls her Tilly. Tilly is very smart. When she sits on Mia's shoulder and Mia talks to her, she nods.

This time, Tilly is not in the garden with the other birds. Mia puts a pinch of millet seeds in her palm and stretches out her arm. "Tilly! Tilly!" she calls, and the bird flies down to her. She lands on Mia's arm and pecks at the seeds. Mia pets her and says, "You are my sweet friend!"

Kai finishes washing the dishes and comes to the garden.

"Can you help me?" Mia asks him.

"Yes, I can help you. Just tell me what you need."

"The roses look so nice today! I want to make a few bouquets and present them to people. Would you give me a hand?"

"With pleasure," says Kai.

They make bouquets, and Kai carries a basket to Central Square. Near the fountain he finds Desi. Kai comes closer to her and sees that her eyes are closed.

This lady is not from our town, he thinks.

"Excuse me, Miss…"

Desi opens her eyes.

"I'm sorry for interrupting your rest. Would you like some flowers? I have yellow roses that match the color of your dress."

Desi looks at him with a smile. "That's so kind of you! Nobody has ever given me flowers before. What is your name, lovely boy?"

"My name is Kai."

"It is a pleasure to meet you, Kai. My name is Desi."

"Are you a guest in our town?" "Yes. I arrived last night." "How do you like it here?" "Oh! I love it!"

"Will you stay?"

"Not for very long. I will go back to my castle soon."

"This is for you," Kai gives Desi the largest bouquet.

Desi takes the flowers and says, "I appreciate your courtesy, Kai, and I'd like to reward you. Do you have a dream?"

"Yes, I do," says Kai.

"What is it?"

"I want to learn how to play the piano."

Desi laughs.

"Why are you laughing, Miss? The only piano in our town is in the Cathedral, and nobody knows how to play it."

"I think I can make your dream come true, Kai. I play the piano, and I can teach you."

"Oh! If you do it, I will be the happiest person in the world!"

"I will, but only on one condition. You must leave Little Town and come with me to my castle. Also, when you know how to play the piano, you will play only for me. Will you come with me, Kai?"

Kai looks at Desi with confusion and remains silent. After a pause he says, "I need to think about it."

"You have only one day to make your decision. My escort will be here soon, and I will be leaving tomorrow."

As they are talking, the service ends in the Cathedral, and the square is filling up with people. Desi stands up from the bench.

"Goodbye, Kai! I hope to see you soon," she says and walks away.

Kai is thinking about Desi's words. Playing the

piano is his cherished dream, but he does not want to desert Mia and grandma. His thoughts are interrupted by an approaching gentleman.

"How much do you want for your roses?" the gentleman asks.

"They are free," says Kai.

"Wonderful! May I take three bouquets for my wife? Today is her birthday."

"Please, help yourself, sir."

The gentleman picks three bouquets of different colors.

Other people also come to Kai to take the flowers. Soon, his basket becomes empty, and he walks home.

Central Square is very crowded now. Shops and restaurants are open, and the smell of cooking makes everyone hungry. Desi stops near a place named the Golden Goose. She walks inside and takes a seat at the table near the window. In an instance, a young woman in a blue apron comes to the table.

"What would you like, Miss?"

"Coffee with cream, and two brioches, please."

"Just a moment," says the waiter and walks to the kitchen. After a minute, she returns with a full tray and sets down a coffee pot, a little jug with cream, and a plate with two brioches.

"Thank you," Desi says. "You're welcome, Miss. Enjoy!"

Desi pours coffee in a cup, adds cream and sugar, and stirs, then she tries a brioche.

"Yummy!" she exclaims. "I have never had anything better!"

When Kai comes home, he goes to his room and shuts the door. He decides not to tell Mia and grandma about his encounter at Central Square. However, Desi's words keep running through his mind. He imagines himself sitting at a big piano and playing it. Suddenly, a knock comes at the door.

"Kai, lunch is ready," Mia says. "I don't feel well," says Kai. "What happened?"

"I have a terrible headache."

"Grandma made creamy potato soup and meatballs."

"I'm not hungry."

"Well, I hope you feel better soon," says Mia and leaves.

Desi enjoys her time in Central Square. In the shops, she finds delightful goodies and meets friendly owners. When the tower clock chimes noon, a cavalcade of twenty horsemen rides into the square. They are all wearing liveries with golden buttons. Behind them, follows a golden carriage drawn by four white horses. This is Desi's escort. The townspeople are astonished: they have never seen such splendor. When the cavalcade stops, the chief horseman plays a bugle. A big crowd surrounds the carriage.

As Desi approaches the cavalcade, the horses bow in reverence. She climbs up to the coachman's seat of the carriage, so that everyone can see her.

"Greetings to you, the dwellers of Little Town!" Desi starts her speech. "I came here last night in the storm tired and hungry, and I found good food and a comfortable bed. Today, I was amazed by your hospitality and all the wonderful work you do. Being a grateful person, I wish to reward you. I invite all of you who know some craft to work for me. I'm a generous person, and I will pay you with pure gold. Whoever wants to go with me, step forward!"

After a few seconds of dead silence, a murmur starts in the throng. It grows louder and louder. Disturbed by Desi's speech, people are discussing her words. Suddenly, Tom, a carpenter and a widower with no children, steps forward.

"I will go with you," he says.

"Welcome!" Desi says.

Then several other men and women approach Desi. Unsurprisingly, all of them are ready to follow her because everyone likes gold.

"My castle is in the mountains beyond the woods," Desi says. "If we leave in the morning, we will arrive there by the end of day. Good night!"

Desi climbs down and gets into the carriage. The cavalcade leaves Central Square for the Fifth Wheel.

The news about Desi and her offer quickly spreads around the town. Many people are tempted to follow her, but their families are not happy because they do not want to be abandoned. Kai, Mia, and Grandma also discuss the news.

"This lady is selfish," Mia says.

"She made an excellent offer," Kai objects. "Whoever works for her will get rich."

"Why do you say this?" Mia says. "Do you know her?"

Kai bows his head in silence.

"What will happen to Little Town?" Grandma sighs.

At night, Kai thinks over and over about Desi's words, but he does not know what the right decision is. He has a strong desire to play the piano, but he does not want to leave Mia and grandma.

Maybe it won't take that long, and I can come back soon, he thinks. *No, I can't desert them! They really need me. I must stay.* The thoughts mingle in Kai's head and keep him from sleeping.

In the morning, the people who want to work for Desi gather in front of the Fifth Wheel. Desi's escort is also there. The chief horseman plays the bugle, and Desi appears at the doors of the tavern. She looks refreshed after a good night sleep.

"Good morning!" she says. "I am glad to see all of you! We are leaving right now."

She gets into the carriage, and the procession hits the road.

Kai and Mia are working in the garden. Kai feels exhausted after his sleepless night. All of a sudden, the children see horsemen riding along the street. A big golden carriage drawn by white horses follows them. In its window, Kai sees Desi. Surprising even himself, Kai runs out to the carriage. Desi opens the door, and the boy jumps inside.

Mia is lost and confused.

"Where are you going, Kai?" she screams. She gets no answer. The carriage disappears at the turn of the road.

Desi is happy to see Kai.

"Congratulations! I think you made the right choice," she says.

The procession leaves the town and enters the woods. All the way to Desi's castle, Kai remains quiet. He feels grateful to her for not asking him questions.

In the evening, the procession reaches the mountains, and on the very top, one can see a castle surrounded by clouds. It looks magnificent and mysterious.

Mia is waiting for Kai to come back. *He won't go far. He will be home by supper*, she thinks.

At sunset, it occurs to her that Kai is probably charmed by the lady and will not return today. She starts crying.

"Please don't cry, my baby!" Grandma comforts her. "You know that Kai loves us. Believe me, my child, he will be home soon."

When Desi and her escort arrive at the castle, she gives orders to the servants. One of them approaches Kai.

"Please follow me, sir," he says.

They go inside, and the servant brings Kai to a room at the end of a long corridor.

"This is your chamber, sir."

Dead tired Kai goes to bed and falls asleep. In the morning, he awakes to a knock at the door.

"Come in!" says Kai, and a maid enters the room.

"Mistress Desi is waiting for you. She wants you to join her for breakfast. Here is some warm water," says the maid and puts a pitcher on the floor.

"I'll be ready in a moment," says Kai. He quickly washes his face and follows the maid.

They climb a few stories and stop in front of a big door. The maid opens it, and Kai walks into a spacious hall. He sees Desi sitting at the end of a long table.

"Good morning, Kai!" she says. "How did you sleep?"

"Very well, Miss, thank you!"

"You can call me simply Desi. I'm very happy to see you. Please have a seat. After breakfast, I will give you a tour of the castle."

Kai is impressed by beautifully set table and Desi's exquisite manners. He is starving but eats very little not to seem rude. After they finish breakfast, Kai follows Desi.

They walk through numerous elegantly furnished rooms, big and small with paintings and tapestries on the walls. One room looks like a huge greenhouse full of exotic plants. Kai leans close to a flower and inhales deeply but does not smell anything.

"Desi, why don't these flowers smell?" he asks.

"They are all manmade," says Desi. "I don't keep live flowers in my castle, because they die."

Another room is a library where the walls are lined with shelves full of books. Kai likes to read, so he asks, "May I read some of these books?"

"You may take any book you like," says Desi. Kai chooses one with a red cover.

Finally, they enter a big room with a piano.

"This is where we will have our lessons," Desi says.

Kai has never been so excited.

"When will we start?" he asks.

"We can start right now," says Desi.

She sits down at the piano and begins playing. She plays well, but the music sounds sad.

In the evening, Kai stays in his room and reads the book he took from the library. It tells about the discovery of a new continent. Suddenly, he thinks of Mia and imagines her face. She is crying. Kai feels heartbroken.

"I have to go back immediately!" he says to himself.

Kai sneaks secretly out of the castle. The late night is lit by a full moon and bright stars.
By dawn, I'll be home! he thinks.

Kai quickly climbs down the rocks and enters the forest. He sees the eyes of wild animals in the bushes and hears the voices of the night birds, but nothing scares the brave boy.

Kai walks all night long. Early in the morning when the sky becomes gray, he finds himself in a small field. *I should be approaching Little Town now*, he thinks. But all he sees is the field and the trees around it. Obviously, he is still deep in the forest. "I'm lost!" he says to himself. Feeling tired he sits down on the grass under a big oak tree to take a rest.

"Good morning, Kai!" says someone.

Kai looks around but sees no one. Suddenly, a big acorn drops on the top of his head. He looks up. A large raven is sitting on a branch.

"Who are you?!" exclaims Kai.

"I am the oldest inhabitant of this forest and a patron of it," the raven says.

"Why are you talking to me?"

"I saw that you were lost, and I wish to help you."

"Help me? How?"

"You are not far from the place you left last night. This path leads straight to the mountains. You must go back and finish what you've started."

"Who do you think you are to tell me what to do?" Kai asks in anger. But he feels exhausted. "Yes, I suppose I will go back. I think I don't have a choice."

At this moment, the sun rises, and its light fills the field. Kai walks back to the castle where he slips in his room. He decides to stay for a little while.

As time goes by, Kai enjoys living in the castle more and more. Desi gives him piano lessons twice a day. Kai is a quick learner. Between lessons, he goes to the library and reads. His favorite books are about travelers and the discoveries of new lands. Sometimes, memories of Mia, Grandma, and their cozy little house with the garden come to his mind, but he tries not to think about them.

Since all the craftsmen have departed, Little Town is not the same anymore. No one builds good houses, no one bakes delicious bread, no one sews comfortable shoes. Travelers stopped visiting this place, and it looks empty. Early winter turns the town into a snowy desert.

Mia and Grandma feel lonely without Kai. The cold weather makes grandma ill. Mia takes good care of her, but the illness is getting worse. Every day, Grandma is weaker and weaker. Mia also brings Tilly the dove into the house to save her from the cold.

One night, the blizzard is so strong that it makes the house squeak. Mia is in the kitchen preparing a special herbal tea with raspberry jam. Grandma always gave this tea to the children when they were sick. Suddenly, Grandma calls Mia. Mia runs to her room and stops in the open doorway.

"Did you call me, Grammy?"

"Mia, my child, please come closer."

When Mia approaches Grandma says, "I won't be here for long."

"What are you talking about?" Mia asks in a quavering voice. "I've just made your special tea. It will give you strength."

"My dear child, please listen to me. You must make Kai come back to Little Town. Write a note to him and Tilly will deliver it. You should both stay together."

After saying this Grandma closes her eyes. Mia shakes her hand and calls to her, but Grandma

remains silent. When Mia understands what has happened, she starts to cry.

In the morning, Mia goes to the Fifth Wheel. Tim is still there. He didn't leave Little Town with the others. In tears, Mia tells him about her loss. Tim comforts the girl. Then he helps bury Grandma.

Mia remembers Grandma's last request, but she decides to wait for warmer weather so that Tilly can fly to Desi's castle safely.

One morning, she hears the sound of dripping water when she wakes up. Mia looks out the window and sees the snow melting under the bright sun.

This is a good day, she thinks. She writes a note to Kai, folds it, ties a ribbon around it in the shape of a tiny necklace, and hangs it on Tilly's neck. Then she plucks a rose from a small potted rose bush and gives it to the dove, who holds the flower in her beak.

 "My little friend," says Mia to the dove, "go to the castle and find Kai!"

Tilly nods. Mia opens the window, and the bird flies away.

When night comes, everyone in the castle is asleep except Kai. He is thinking about Mia and Grandma. He feels that he made a big mistake and lost a priceless treasure. Suddenly, he hears a little noise. He looks at the window and sees a dove standing on the still. The bird is holding a red rose in her beak.

"Tilly!" exclaims Kai. He opens the window and lets the bird in. He sees a note. He takes it off the Tilly's neck, unfolds it, and reads: "I love you. Please come back."

Kai's eyes fill with tears. He runs to the hall with the piano, opens all the windows, and starts playing.

A charming and magnificent music spreads through the castle. It goes to every room. Kai plays from the bottom of his heart, sharing his passion. When he stops, the rising sun floods the hall with bright light.

At that moment, Desi runs into the hall.

"You broke my rule!" she exclaims.

"I have to go back to Little Town," says Kai.

"Why? Aren't you happy here?" says Desi.

"Yes and no," says Kai. "I enjoy staying in your castle, but I left in Little Town someone I love."

For an instant, Desi looks angry and then she looks sad.

"Before you go, I want to tell you my story," she says.

"I'm listening," says Kai.

"Many years ago, there lived a boy and a girl named Peter and Veronica. They lived in a beautiful land surrounded by meadows and lakes. Peter's father was a farmer, and Veronica's mother was a piano teacher. The children loved each other from an early age. When they were ten years old, their parents engaged them, and when they were fifteen, Peter married Veronica. They were a happy couple. Peter worked with his father on the farm, and Veronica composed music. Only one thing made them sorrowful—they had no children.

"One day, Peter's father died, and soon after that Veronica's mother passed away. A year later, Veronica found out that she was expecting a child. Peter was so happy that he planted a beautiful garden in front of their house. The baby was born on a frosty winter morning. Veronica was very weak after the delivery, and three days later she died. After losing his wife, Peter was devastated, and it was very difficult for him to take care of the baby alone. His uncle George took him and the baby to his castle where many servants could help.

"Veronica and Peter were my parents, and the baby was me. For the most part, I was a happy child, except I missed my mother, whom I had never seen but knew about from my father. In the winter, we lived in the castle. In the summer, my father took me back to his farm. Uncle George honored my mother's memory by hiring a talented musician to teach me to play the piano.

"When I became a young lady, my father and granduncle tried to find me a husband. Many families visited the castle to introduce their sons to me, but I did not want to leave my father. I was eighteen, when uncle George passed away, because he was very old. He had no children and bequeathed all his property to me. My father was not that old, but he did not live much longer. Last winter he died too, and I was left alone."

Desi pauses for a moment and then says with a deep sigh:

"This is my story, Kai."

"It is a sad story," says Kai. "I wish I could stay with you, but I do have to leave."

"Will I see you again?"
"I don't know."

"You can't leave me like this after all I've done for you!" exclaims Desi angrily.

"Dear Desi, you don't look pretty when you're angry," Kai says with a sad smile. "You shared your story with me. Now please listen to mine."

"I've lived in Little Town since I was five. Grandma brought me and Mia there from a big city standing on the bank of a broad river with a huge port full of ships. Mia's father and my father were friends from childhood. Since youth, they had been dreaming of building a ship and traveling across the ocean. When they grew up, they married two young ladies who were cousins. Mia and I were born just one month apart.

"Soon after that, my mother's father, grandpa John, paid for a ship as a gift to our fathers and hired them a crew. In early spring, when Mia and I had just turned four our parents eagerly set sail on a voyage. On the day of their departure, a big crowd gathered at the port. An orchestra played marches, and people threw flowers before the procession of nobles who joined the expedition.

"Since then, no one heard from the ship. Hardly handling his grief, grandpa John asked Mia's grandmother to raise me and Mia, and she brought us to her house in Little Town."

Kai stops talking; his eyes are wet. Desi remains silent, but her face shows compassion.

"You should go home, Kai," she says after a pause.

"Thank you for everything you have done for me!" says Kai.

Desi covers her face with her hands and runs out of the room. Kai pets Tilly who is sitting on his shoulder.

"Don't worry, sweetie. We will go home soon." Tilly nods.

This morning, people from Little Town who work in the castle gathered to discuss a dream they all had last night. In this dream, everyone heard majestic music and saw their town surrounded by the desert.

Paul, a baker, says, "Listen, brothers! We should go back."

Some people agree, but others want to stay because they like living in the castle. While they discuss it, Kai shows up.

He stands before them and speaks loudly:

"Citizens of Little Town! Do you remember how happy we were there? Our families need us! We should go back and make Little Town better than it was! We can do it easily now with all the money we have."

Everyone starts talking, and all the voices merge into one loud noise. When the noise quiets down Kai continues,

"I am leaving today. Who will come with me?"

"I will," says an old lady.

Then everyone says, "Me too," – all except Tom, the carpenter, who was the first to join Desi.

After the meeting, the townspeople pack their belongings and leave the castle. Kai walks ahead of them with a servant of Desi who shows them the way.

It is spring. The snow has melted, and the air is very fresh. The first flowers can be seen on the ground, and the birds are singing.

By midnight, they reach Little Town. Kai approaches their house. He sees a light in the window. When he walks inside, he finds Mia sitting in the kitchen. She has stayed up late waiting for Tilly. When she sees Kai, her face becomes radiant, and she smiles.

"Where is Grandma?" asks Kai. Mia bursts into tears.

Kai hugs her and says, "Show me where."

They both go to the cemetery. The grave still looks fresh. It has wild violets blooming around it.

"Memory eternal!" says Kai.

The next day, all the townspeople gather in the Cathedral for the service in memory of Gloria, Mia's grandmother. Kai plays a requiem on the piano.

After the service, Mia and Kai walk home. They pass through the streets and talk. Kai holds Mia's hand for the first time since coming back.

"You played beautifully today," says Mia. "Who was your teacher?"

"Desi," says Kai.

"That selfish rich lady?!" Mia exclaims in anger.

"She is a nice person, but she is very lonely. She lost her mother when she was only three days old. Now, after her father has also died, she is an orphan."

"Like us," says Mia sadly.

"Yes," says Kai. "She told me her story. We have many things in common."

"Maybe," says Mia. "But it's because of her that we lost our Grandma!"

"Don't say this Mia, please," says Kai in a soft voice. "You are very kind, and I think we could be good friends with Desi."

"No way!" exclaims Mia. "I will never go to her castle!"

"You don't have to. Desi will come to Little Town."

"What will she do here?"

"She will teach children how to play the piano."

"Ah. Maybe it is a good idea," says Mia, musingly.

When the children walk by the lake, they stop for a moment to watch the sunset. All of a sudden, Kai turns and looks at Mia's face. Her big green eyes are full of soft light.

"What is it, Kai?" Mia asks in a tender voice.

"Will you marry me?" asks Kai.

Mia smiles and says, "Yes!" Then she adds, "But we are too young…"

"We can wait until we are older," says Kai.

"Let's go home!" Mia says laughing. "Tilly is waiting for us."

Tilly now lives in a golden cage, a gift from Desi. During the week, Mia and Kai work around the house, which is old and needs a lot of repairs. On Sundays, Kai plays the piano in the Cathedral. All the people of Little Town work very hard to make their place better. Everybody is happy again.

Only Desi is unhappy. She no longer enjoys living in the castle with her servants. She thinks about Kai. One Sunday morning, she comes to Little Town and goes to the Cathedral. It is the middle of the service, and Kai is playing. When he sees Desi, he starts playing the best music he has learned.

After the service ends, Desi approaches Kai. "I've missed you," she says.

"I've missed you too," says Kai. "Welcome back."

Kai invites Desi to his house, and they have lunch with Mia.

After lunch, he shows her the garden.

"Your garden reminds me of the one at my father's farm," says Desi, "I have not been at that place since his death. Will you and Mia join me if I go there?"

"Yes, we definitely will," says Kai.

"Good. It's time for me to leave," Desi says, "But I wish I could stay."

"You can," says Kai.

Desi looks at Kai with surprise, "What would I do here?"

"You can teach children to play the piano. You are an excellent teacher."

"I might agree. But I need to think about it," says Desi.

Kai walks her to the gate, where one of her servants is waiting with two horses. Desi and her servant mount for the ride.

"Goodbye, Kai! Thank you for your hospitality!" she says.

"You are very welcome, Desi!" says Kai.

A week later, Desi returns. Since then, she visits Little Town every Sunday to give piano lessons, and the children enjoy them greatly. During the week, Desi stays in her castle or at her father's farm. Mia and Kai often travel to the farm to see her, and she treats them as guests of honor.

In a year, Little Town becomes an oasis. Many new children are born. All the people enjoy living in wellness, prosperity, peace, and love.

www.ingramcontent.com/pod-product-compliance
Lightning Source LLC
Chambersburg PA
CBHW040312180626
46815CB00015B/38